THIS WALKER BOOK BELONGS TO:

_____

_____

_____

Dog Blue

YAP!

Polly Dunbar

Bertie loved blue.

He had a blue
jumper,

a blue dog
collar,

blue shoes,

but no blue dog.

What Bertie wanted

more than anything in the

whole wide world was a dog.

A blue dog!

So Bertie pretended
he had a blue dog.

He patted his
pretend blue dog.

He fed his pretend
blue dog.

He took his pretend
blue dog for a walk.

He threw a stick for
his pretend blue dog.

But pretend dogs don't fetch sticks.

So Bertie fetched the stick himself.

Bertie pretended
he was a dog,
a blue dog.

He scratched
like a blue dog.

He sniffed
like a blue dog.

He chased his
tail like
a blue
dog.

And Bertie yapped like a blue dog.

YAP!

A
real dog
yapped
back!

A tiny dog,

all alone
and looking for
an owner.

A black and
white dog.

A beautiful,
spotty dog.

A perfect dog.

Bertie's dog!

But hang on ...

wait a moment ...

Bertie's
dog isn't
blue at
all!

Bertie thought and thought.
If this black and white,
beautiful, spotty,

perfect dog

were his dog

but not a

blue

dog ...

then he must give the dog something blue ...

a name!

BLUE!

Bertie called his dog Blue.

What a perfect pair!

Bertie took Blue for a walk.

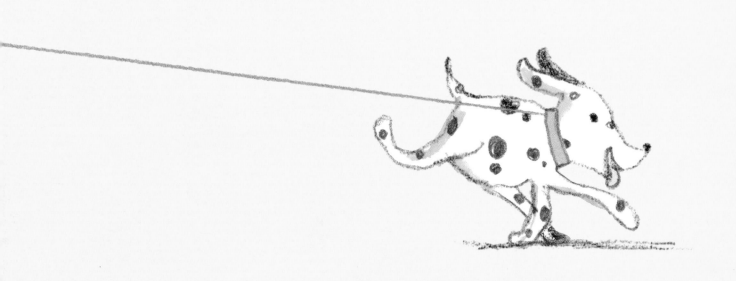

Blue took Bertie for a walk.

Bertie fed Blue.

Blue sniffed Bertie.

Bertie patted Blue.

Blue wagged his tail.

Then Blue
showed Bertie how
tail-chasing is done,
when you're a real dog
and you really
have a
tail.

So Bertie doesn't
need to pretend any more.

Blue really loves Bertie.

Bertie really loves Blue.

Especially when ...

it's Bertie's turn to fetch!

WALKER BOOKS is the world's leading
independent publisher of children's books.
Working with the best authors and illustrators
we create books for all ages, from babies
to teenagers – books your child will
grow up with and always remember. So…

FOR THE BEST CHILDREN'S BOOKS,
LOOK FOR THE BEAR